This book belongs to

THE BABY'S
Playtime

Book

Kay Chorao

Dutton Children's Books

For Sadie

DUTTON CHILDREN'S BOOKS
A division of Penguin Young Readers Group
Published by the Penguin Group • Penguin Group (USA) Inc., 375 Hudson Street, New York, New York 10014, U.S.A.
Penguin Group (Canada), 90 Eglinton Avenue East, Suite 700, Toronto, Ontario, Canada M4P 2Y3 (a division of Pearson Penguin Canada Inc.) •
Penguin Books Ltd, 80 Strand, London WC2R 0RL, England • Penguin Ireland, 25 St Stephen's Green, Dublin 2, Ireland (a division of Penguin Books Ltd)
• Penguin Group (Australia), 250 Camberwell Road, Camberwell, Victoria 3124, Australia (a division of Pearson Australia Group Pty Ltd) • Penguin Books
India Pvt Ltd, 11 Community Centre, Panchsheel Park, New Delhi - 110 017, India • Penguin Group (NZ), Cnr Airborne and Rosedale Roads, Albany,
Auckland 1310, New Zealand (a division of Pearson New Zealand Ltd) • Penguin Books (South Africa) (Pty) Ltd, 24 Sturdee Avenue, Rosebank, Johannesburg
2196, South Africa • Penguin Books Ltd, Registered Offices: 80 Strand, London WC2R 0RL, England

Every attempt has been made to trace the ownership of all copyrighted material and to secure the necessary permissions
to reprint these selections. In the event of any question arising as to the use of any material, the editor and the publisher,
while expressing regret for any inadvertent error, will be happy to make the necessary correction in future printings.
The publisher gratefully acknowledges the right to reprint:

"Doll," copyright © 1985 by Myra Cohn Livingston.
Reprinted with the permission of Margaret K. McElderry Books, an imprint of Simon & Schuster
Children's Publishing Division, from *Worlds I Know and Other Poems* by Myra Cohn Livingston.

"Blowing Bubbles" by Margaret Hillert. Used by permission of the author, who controls all rights.

"Push—Pull" by Robert Morrow. Used by permission of the author, who controls all rights.

Illustrations copyright © 2006 by Kay Sproat Chorao

Library of Congress Cataloging-in-Publication Data

The baby's playtime book / [compiled by] Kay Chorao.— 1st ed.
p. cm.
ISBN 0-525-47576-1
1. Play—Juvenile poetry. 2. Children's poetry, American. 3. Nursery rhymes, American. I. Chorao, Kay.
PS595.P6B33 2006
811.008'357—dc22
2005009906

Published in the United States by Dutton Children's Books,
a division of Penguin Young Readers Group, 345 Hudson Street, New York, New York 10014
www.penguin.com

Designed by Irene Vandervoort

Manufactured in China   First Edition
1 3 5 7 9 10 8 6 4 2

~ Contents ~

ALL THE WORLD'S A STAGE

All the world's a stage,
And all the men and women
merely players.

~ *William Shakespeare*

WHISKERS MEETS POLLY

Razzle Dazzle!
    She's so fine!
All dressed up
    Like a diamond mine!

So much glass!
    So much glitter!
Bright red dress
    That doesn't fit her.

       ～ *Michael Stillman*

WILD BEASTS

I will be a lion
    And you shall be a bear,
And each of us will have a den
    Beneath a nursery chair;
And you must growl and growl and growl,
    And I will roar and roar,
And then—why, then—you'll growl again,
    And I will roar some more!

~ *Evaleen Stein*

WE'RE OFF!

We're off,
We're off,
We're off in a motorcar.
The lion and bear are after us,
THE LION AND BEAR ARE AFTER US,
And they don't know where we are.

Traditional (adapted by Kay Chorao)

THE TEDDY BEARS' PICNIC

If you go down in the woods today,
You're sure of a big surprise.
If you go down in the woods today,
You'd better go in disguise.

For every bear that ever there was
Will gather there, for certain, because
Today's the day the teddy bears have
their picnic.

~ Jimmy Kennedy

DOLLY'S NEW DRESS

I like to make clothes for my dolly,
  I make all of her dresses, you know.
I pick out the fabric and cut it,
  And with needle and thread, I will sew.

I fit it and tuck it and hem it,
  And sew little buttons on too.
And Dolly is always so happy
  When she puts on a dress that is new.

~ *Ernest Nister*

THERE WAS A LITTLE GIRL

There was a little girl who had a little curl
Right in the middle of her forehead;
And when she was good she was very, very good,
But when she was bad she was horrid.

~ Henry Wadsworth Longfellow

DANCE TO YOUR DADDY

Dance to your daddy,
  My little babby,
Dance to your daddy,
  My little lamb.

You shall have a fishy
  In a little dishy,
You shall have a fishy
  When the boat comes in.

You shall have an apple,
  You shall have a plum,
You shall have a rattle-basket
  When your daddy comes home.

ENGINE, ENGINE

Engine, Engine number nine,
Going down the railroad line.
If the train goes off the track,
Do you want your money back?

PUSH—PULL

I *push* my truck—
Away it goes.
I *pull* my truck—
Look out, toes!

~ *Rob Morrow*

~ 15 ~

GRANDMA'S SPECTACLES

These are Grandma's spectacles.
This is Grandma's hat.
This is the way she folds her hands
And puts them in her lap.

I'M A LITTLE TEAPOT

I'm a little teapot,
Short and stout.
Here is my handle,
Here is my spout.
When the tea is ready,
Hear me shout.
Tip me over and
Pour me out.

DAFFY DOWN DILLY

Daffy Down Dilly
Has come to town
In a yellow petticoat
And a green gown.

SAND CASTLES

We take our shoes and stockings off
And play barefoot in the sand.
Then with our shovels and pails we build
A castle that's truly grand.

∽ *Ernest Nister*

SAILING

There's never a boat that sails the sea,
    With a crew so merry and brave as we.
Our oars go up, and our oars go down,
    And we're many a mile away from town.

Ernest Nister

THE ITSY BITSY SPIDER

The itsy bitsy spider
Climbed up the waterspout.
Down came the rain
And washed the spider out.
Out came the sun
And dried up all the rain.
And the itsy bitsy spider
Climbed up the spout again.

IN GRANDPA'S BARN

In Grandpa's barn on a rainy day,
We swung on ropes; we sailed away.

In Grandpa's barn on a rainy day,
We climbed on stalls; we fed the bay.

In Grandpa's barn on a rainy day,
We found a surprise in the prickly hay.

In Grandpa's barn on a rainy day,
Four tiny kittens asleep where they lay.

N. Luka

A CAT CAME FIDDLING

A cat came fiddling out of a barn
With a pair of bagpipes under her arm.
She could sing nothing but fiddle-dee-dee,
The mouse has married the bumblebee.
Pipe, cat; dance, mouse;
We'll have a wedding at our good house.

MY AUNT JANE

My aunt Jane,
She came from France
To teach to me the polka dance.
First the heel,
And then the toe—
That's the way
The dance should go.

I DANCED WITH THE GIRL

I danced with the girl
With a hole in her stocking,
And her heel kept a-knocking,
And her toes kept a-rocking,
I danced with the girl
With a hole in her stocking,
And we danced by the light of the moon.

RIDE AWAY

Ride away, ride away,
    Johnny shall ride,
And he shall have pussy-cat
    Tied to one side;
And he shall have little dog
    Tied to the other,
And Johnny shall ride
    To see his grandmother.

THIS IS THE WAY THE LADIES RIDE

This is the way the ladies ride,
        Nim, nim, nim, nim.
This is the way the gentlemen ride,
        Trim, trim, trim, trim.
This is the way the farmers ride,
        Trot, trot, trot, trot.
This is the way the huntsmen ride,
        A-gallup, a-gallup, a-gallup, a-gallup.
This is the way the ploughboys ride,
        Hobble-dy-gee, hobble-dy-gee.

MUD

Mud is very nice to feel
All squishy-squash between the toes!
I'd rather wade in wiggly mud
Than smell a yellow rose.

Nobody else but the rosebush knows
How nice mud feels
Between the toes.

~ Polly Chase Boyden

BLOWING BUBBLES

Dip your pipe and gently blow.
Watch the tiny bubble grow
Big and bigger, round and fat,
Rainbow-colored, and then—
SPLAT!

~ *Margaret Hillert*

SEE HOW I'M JUMPING

See how I'm jumping, jumping, jumping;
See how I'm bouncing like a ball.

I never knew I could jump so high.
I never knew I could touch the sky.

See how I'm jumping, jumping, jumping.
When I get tired, I fall down!

JACK-IN-A-BOX

If I were a Jack-in-a-box,
I'd make myself very small.
I'd be shut tight inside my box.
You couldn't see me at all.
Until someone turns the crank,
The music will play—then stop,
The top will fly open,
And out I'll pop!

DOLL

The Christmas
when my sister came

she got a doll
without a name

and so I helped her out
and chose

Samantha

and put on her clothes
and dressed her up
and curled her hair.
I took Samantha everywhere

and hid her underneath the bed
so she could be my doll instead.

~ *Myra Cohn Livingston*

OH, PLAYMATE

Oh, playmate,
Come out and play with me,
And bring your dollies three,
Climb up my apple tree.
Look down my rain barrel,
Slide down my cellar door,
And we'll be jolly friends
Forever more.

⁓ Saxie Dowell

NOISE

Billy is blowing his trumpet;
Bertie is banging a tin;
Betty is crying for Mummy,
And Bob has pricked Ben with a pin.
Baby is crying out loudly;
He's out on the lawn in his pram.
I am the only one silent,
And I've eaten all of the jam.

~ *Anonymous*

JOHNNY

To Johnny a box
is a house
or a car
or a ship
or a train
or a horse.
A stick
is a sword
or a spear
or a cane,
and a carpet
is magic
of course.

~ *Marci Ridlon*

MY SHADOW

I have a little shadow that goes in and out with me,
And what can be the use of him is more than I can see.
He is very, very like me from the heels up to the head;
And I see him jump before me, when I jump into my bed.
The funniest thing about him is the way he likes to grow—
Not at all like proper children, which is always very slow;
For he sometimes shoots up taller like an india-rubber ball,
And he sometimes gets so little that there's none of him at all.

∾ *Robert Louis Stevenson*

A KITE

I often sit and wish that I
Could be a kite up in the sky,
And ride upon the breeze and go
Whichever way I chanced to blow.

∾ *Anonymous*

THE SWING

How do you like to go up in a swing,
   Up in the air so blue?
Oh, I do think it the pleasantest thing
   Ever a child can do!

   Up in the air and over the wall,
      Till I can see so wide,
   River and trees and cattle and all
      Over the countryside—

      Till I look down on the garden green,
         Down on the roof so brown—
      Up in the air I go flying again,
         Up in the air and down!

~ *Robert Louis Stevenson*

~ 35 ~

MISS LUCY HAD A BABY

Miss Lucy had a baby,
She named him Tiny Tim.
She put him in the bathtub
To see if he could swim.

He drank up all the water,
He ate up all the soap.
He tried to eat the bathtub,
But it wouldn't go down his throat.

Miss Lucy called the doctor.
Miss Lucy called the nurse.
Miss Lucy called the lady
With the alligator purse.

"Measles," said the doctor.
"Mumps," said the nurse.
"Nothing," said the lady
With the alligator purse.

Miss Lucy kicked the doctor.
Miss Lucy slapped the nurse.
Miss Lucy paid the lady
With the alligator purse.

‿ Traditional

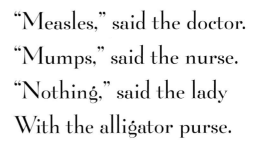

IN WINTER

Watch me, watch me on the ice.
Watch me spin, I'll do it twice.
But sometimes when I circle round,
My feet fly up and I fall down!

~ N. Luka

DOWN THE SLIPPERY SLIDE

Down the slippery slide they slid
Sitting slightly sideways;
Slipping swiftly see them skid
On holidays and Fridays.

~ Anonymous

THE MORE WE GET TOGETHER

The more we get together, together, together,
The more we get together, the happier we'll be.
For your friends are my friends
And my friends are your friends.
The more we get together, the happier we'll be.

~ Anonymous